John Bell

Medical Heroism

Anatiposi

John Bell

Medical Heroism

Reprint of the original.

1st Edition 2023 | ISBN: 978-3-38230-130-9

Anatiposi Verlag is an imprint of Outlook Verlagsgesellschaft mbH.

Verlag (Publisher): Outlook Verlag GmbH, Zeilweg 44, 60439 Frankfurt, Deutschland
Vertretungsberechtigt (Authorized to represent): E. Roepke, Zeilweg 44, 60439 Frankfurt, Deutschland
Druck (Print): Books on Demand GmbH, In de Tarpen 42, 22848 Norderstedt, Deutschland

Medical Heroism.

ADDRESS

PHILADELPHIA COUNTY MEDICAL SOCIETY,

DELIVERED

FEBRUARY 24, 1859.

BY

JOHN BELL, M. D.,

AT THE CLOSE OF HIS OFFICIAL TERM AS PRESIDENT.

PUBLISHED BY ORDER OF THE SOCIETY.

PHILADELPHIA:
COLLINS, PRINTER, 705 JAYNE STREET.
1859.

Medical Heroism.

ADDRESS

BEFORE THE

PHILADELPHIA COUNTY MEDICAL SOCIETY,

DELIVERED

FEBRUARY 24, 1859.

BY

JOHN BELL, M. D.,

AT THE CLOSE OF HIS OFFICIAL TERM AS PRESIDENT.

PUBLISHED BY ORDER OF THE SOCIETY.

PHILADELPHIA:
COLLINS, PRINTER, 705 JAYNE STREET.
1859.

ADDRESS.

OUR Society requires that its President shall deliver a public address at the close of his term of office. He is, of course, free to select his subject. It may be treated in a strain of advice or of encouragement, of warning, or even of reprehension; provided, always, that it be clothed in the language of sincerity and good-will. The science, the art, the literature, and the ethics of medicine, furnish numerous themes for copious and learned, and even eloquent discourse. It has fallen to my lot, during a tolerably long and not idle life, to glean something from the various fields in our professional domain; and I might, perhaps, without presumption, make an offering to you, at this time, of some of these gatherings. But why should I attempt to indoctrinate those who are, as their title implies, already *docti*, learned men; or to penetrate into the mysteries of science, and to portray its diversified aspects and relations to those who, with microscope armed, can see through and through an object, and enjoy the additional privilege of afterwards reasoning round and round about it? Who shall say where the homologous ends and the heterologous begins? Some histologists are now inclined to question the correctness of the sentence of outlawry pressed against certain diseased textures, just as some historians would plead an arrest of judgment on certain personages who have always been spoken and written of in terms of execration. We are told, for example, that the terrible cancer itself, which but yesterday, as it were, was declared to display its virulence, not only on its face, but in its ultimate cells, is, to-day, alleged to have no such special characteristics, and that its cells are merely deformed homologous ones. So, in reference to some historical names—Tiberius, Richard III., and, just now, Henry VIII. We learn, as the result of more careful investigations, that these much abused gentlemen were full of good intentions, not, in truth, well understood, and which had, somehow or another, gone astray. We are everywhere met by contrasts which, in the self-sufficiency of half-knowledge, we call contradictions. Bile and sugar are now found to keep company together, and even to be elaborated by the same organ, so that the old comparison— bitter as gall—must henceforth be qualified with the addition—but with a touch of the saccharine. It must have been by a psychological analysis, conducted in a similar method, that the sweet part in the character of the tyrants just named has been discovered by their respective apologists. A history of the functions of the human organism would show almost as many changes and revolutions as general history does of successions of dynasties and overthrows of empires; both of them having their mythical as well as their proper historic periods. Scarcely, for example, have we become accustomed to hear of pepsin and the part which it is assumed to perform in digestion, as well as that other, by which it is made to figure in the advertisements and placards of lying quacks, who cannot tell the difference between pepsin and pepper, when we are presented with pancreatin. Hitherto the pancreatic juice was believed to be analogous to saliva, and to hold quite a subsidiary office in digestion. Now, through its active principle, pancreatin, it is invested with properties by which a common eater, who takes a dose of it, will be able to rival the gastronomic feats of a London alderman, or that more diminutive, but not less decided glutton, the hydra, which is all stomach. If the luxurious and degenerate Romans, under the empire, had known of the existence of this little polype and of its wonderful powers, they would have deified it, and placed its magnified image at the head of their supper-tables. They endeavored to renew the pleasures of eating by taking an emetic, and thus making room for a second repast immediately after the first. The hydra can, as you know, do this and more besides; not only can it disgorge itself of its prey, but, if turned inside out, as you would the finger of a glove, what was before skin becomes stomach, and is as eager for food and as ready to digest it, as was its legitimate predecessor, which is now metamorphosed into skin.

When we speak of changes and transference of attributes, our minds immediately turn to the nervous system, and especially to the spinal marrow and the great sympathetic, which, although it is

by no means a *terra incognita*, is still to physiologists what Central
Africa has been to ethnologists and geographers—a wide field of
discovery and no little speculation. For a while we were allowed
to settle down into a belief in the conclusions reached by Sir
Charles Bell and by Magendie, on the functions of the spinal marrow; but we are all again at sea, watching the pilotings and sound-
ings of men of another generation, who are as busy and industrious,
and quite as confident of the truth of their views, as were their
immediate predecessors.

Progress, change, reform, and improvement are the watchwords
of the day, saving and excepting always in as far as medical education is concerned. Our medical schools constitute no exception
to the universal experience, that corporations never reform themselves, are never the leaders, but always the opposers of innovation,
which in their ears sounds like revolution and anarchy. Nearly a
century has elapsed since the first medical school in the then British
Provinces of North America was founded (1765), in the city of
Philadelphia, by Dr. John Morgan and Dr. William Shippen, with
whom were associated, ere long, Dr. Adam Kuhn, Dr. Thomas
Bond, Dr. Benjamin Rush, and, at later dates, Dr. James T. Hutch-
inson, Dr. Samuel Powell Griffiths, Dr. Caspar Wistar, and Dr.
Benj. Smith Barton, and in the early part of the present century
(1805), Dr. Philip Syng Physick. During all this time the curri-
culum of medical studies has undergone little change, and then not
always for the better. There have been more curtailments of the
original scheme of instruction than additions to it. The chair of
clinical medicine, filled first by Dr. Bond, and afterwards by Dr.
Rush, has, since then, been thrust to one side: that of natural history and botany was never occupied except by Dr. Barton, before
he was transferred to the chair of materia medica and botany. All
the additions made to the first plan have been, not of branches, but
of separate chairs for different branches, which used to be taught
from one chair. The medical schools which, in succession, have
been organized in different parts of the United States since the
creation of that of the old Philadelphia College, afterwards merged
into the University of Pennsylvania, have taken it as their model;
and now, forsooth, in the entire length and breadth of the land, we
are to content ourselves with a course of medical instruction, which,
as measured by subjects or branches in the middle of the nineteenth
century, was not deemed to be more than barely requisite to meet

the wants of the middle of the eighteenth. Branches of medicine which were then merely sketched have been filled up since to the extent of a hundred-fold, and new ones have been opened out; but still, no practical acknowledgment of the fact is made by a proportionately increased number of teachers, and scarcely any by an increase of the period in which they are to lecture. With a hundred-fold more positive facts pertaining to every branch of medicine, and a hundred-fold more experiments for their illustration and enforcement, the collegiate term allowed for the introduction and arrangement of these facts, and the making of these experiments, is, with a very few honorable exceptions, as brief as ever. The inference from this state of things is obvious. They who wish to obtain the full, or rather a liberal measure of medical attainments, must prosecute their studies outside of college walls. Within these walls they cannot expect to receive methodical instruction in hygiene, public and private, botany, pathological anatomy, pathology in its large and recognized meaning, medical jurisprudence, medical biography, including the history of medicine; nor, finally, in medical bibliography. As far as collegiate instruction goes, we are quite unprepared to appear before the courts of law, and to give our testimony clearly and with understanding on questions which affect the reputation, the fortunes, and the lives of our fellow citizens—questions which belong to medical jurisprudence, or legal medicine, as it is often termed. It would be thought strange for a politician, who aspires to figure in public life, to be ignorant of the history of his own country, or even of general history. What shall we say of the alumni of our medical schools being sent abroad into the world, in ignorance of the history of medicine, its successive improvements, and the causes which at different times retarded its progress, as well as of the distinctive merits of those eminent men who have enlarged the boundaries of medical science, or made improvements in medical art? It may be grating to our national vanity, which certainly is not small, for us to be told that, in the matter of medical education, Young America has yet much to learn from Old Europe; but, unfortunately for us, the averment is undoubtedly true.

All honor and renown, then, to those noble men who forego the distinctions conferred by office and the emoluments from practice in the eager search after and discovery of new facts, and the developing of accordant principles. They dig the gold, not always caring themselves to convert it into crowns for kings and current coin for the people: they find the rich material for others to decorate themselves with. The world would hold of small account the common sense of those who, calling themselves utilitarians, should cry out to the patient delvers and miners of the precious metals: "We do not want your gold-dust or your lumps, or even ingots; give us something we can apply to purposes of use and ornament —vessels of various sizes and shapes, rings, brooches, clasps, chains, chased work, not to speak of plate for the table." The medical philosopher might ask: "Is there more wisdom in the cant of the day among many practitioners of medicine, who are continually calling for the practical, not as the crowning capital of the column of medical science, but rather, according to their notion, as a separate block, almost as rough as when taken from the quarry, but whose surface has been hacked by random strokes of common workmen, each leaving his mark, and calling it his experience." What long and patient delving into the interior of the human frame! What careful observation of the structure and connections of the several parts of which it is composed! What nice induction was exercised before an approach could be made to a knowledge of the uses and combined action of these several parts! Observation, experiment, hypothesis, theory, were each invoked in turn before the meaning of what passes in the interior could be read on the surface, before the elaborated vital manifestations could be appreciated by and made serviceable to the practical physician.

The practical man may be heard to boast that he contents himself, in the treatment of disease, with noting the symptoms and prescribing the remedies which experience has shown to be most available for the removal of those symptoms. But, during this time, he seems to forget that he is not dealing with separate phenomena, ultimate facts, which have no special connection with or relation to one another, and require no chain of theory to unite them together. That of which the senses take direct cognizance is indeed a matter of fact, such as the color and coating of the tongue, the physical qualities of the pulse, &c.; but the meaning, semeiologically considered, of these appearances and states, is a question of theory, respecting which we cannot speak with certainty, inasmuch as the precise relation between the phenomena observed and the state of the internal organs, of which the former are supposed to be the representation, the symptoms, in fine, is not equally demonstrable to the senses, is not a matter of simple legitimate experience. A practical physician, so called, will say, that a yellow and loaded tongue indicates bilious disorder, and that such is his experience; that is to say, that he was taught this symptomatology, and continues to believe it. From this belief, he deduces his practice of giving a mercurial purgative.

But, may not more careful observation show that all this so called experience, this alleged dealing in matter-of-fact, is false reasoning—is false theory; and that the stomach, not the liver, is in fault, and that a day's fasting, and the use of diluent drinks, may well be substituted for purging? There is not a single symptom to which a practitioner of medicine attaches any value that does not call on the intellect to trace in it a cause and an effect, and to deduce from this connection, be it real or be it supposititious, a new condition of things; in fine, a theory. How much more than theoretical, how purely speculative must be that so-called experience which rests on conclusions from obvious phenomena, the inner or remoter causes of which are conjectured or unknown! Your mere practical man feels, for example, the pulse of his patient, with a desire of ascertaining whether the latter has fever; and he thinks he is no theorist if, at the same time, he avoids all discussion or inquiry into the proximate cause and nature of fever. It does not occur to him that in the very use of the term fever, he gives into an abstraction, and deals with a theory of the most complex kind. But waiving this point, he may, perhaps, assure us that the pulse, whose beats, and their force and regularity, or intermission, are matters of certainty, furnishes him with most reliable indications of the intensity and the degree of the fever. He has no doubts on this head; he confidently rests his belief on experience. But, to what does this experience amount? It is neither more nor less than a repetition for a lengthened period of a theory, which supposes that certain physical characters of the pulse are caused by, or indicate those complex and unknown changes in the functions of the organism, designated by the abstract term fever.

During the long period of nineteen centuries, or from the time of Herophilus, of Alexandria, who was the first to speak of the arterial pulse, and of Praxagoras, who first gave it diagnostic value, down to the date of the discovery of the circulation of the blood by Harvey, physicians, practised ones, too, spoke and argued with confidence of the diagnostic and prognostic value of sphygmology, although they were long ignorant of the very first step in the real process of causation—viz., the anatomical connection between the arteries and the heart, and that the pulsations of the former are the effect of the contractions of the latter organ acting on the contained blood while circulating in elastic vessels. Galen, coming four centuries later than Herophilus, taught that pulsations were caused by the vital forces, and that the heart, through the *pneuma*, communicated the pulsatile faculty to the arteries. He supposed the pulse to be an index to the vital forces, and, as such, that it pointed out, not only the character of the disease, but its probable termination, either in recovery or in death. He went farther, and invested the pulse with the function of preserving the animal heat, of drawing in cold air, and of discharging effete matters from the blood. Galen wrote a complete course of sphygmology, divided into four sections, each including four books, besides several monographs on the same subject. In his first book, he enumerates more than sixty varieties of pulse, each having its distinct or diagnostic character, and indicating a particular disease. Hence, there was assumed to be a pleuritic pulse, a suppurative pulse, a phthisical pulse, an hepatic pulse, a splenic pulse, &c. In these refinements, the teacher of Pergamos has found imitators among the moderns, and especially among the French physicians of the last century. For the next fifteen hundred years, or almost until the discovery of the circulation of the blood, the Galenical doctrines of the pulse were taught in the schools, and received by practitioners of medicine as their guide in semeiotics. When Harvey appeared, and the true mechanical cause of the pulse was ascertained to be the contractile power of the heart and elasticity of the arteries, which last were no longer believed to contain vital spirits or air, in addition to blood, the practical men of the day must have thought themselves aggrieved at a discovery which would require them to begin their experience anew, and to reach conclusions so different from those which had previously satisfied them.

With the predominance of the iatro-mathematical school, and the explaining of the circulation of the blood and of other fluids of the living body by the laws of hydraulics, the pulse came to assume new and different significations from those that had been attached to it by the followers of Galen. Although called an eclectic, the eminent Boerhaave belonged to this school, and through his teaching, its doctrines, during a considerable part of the last century, were disseminated, and generally adopted throughout Europe and in English America, as far as this country possessed at the time educated physicians. When, afterwards, by the labors of Stahl, Frederick Hoffman, and, above all, the lucid prelections of Cullen, vitalism, and with it solidism, obtained the ascendency, how many wise doctors shook their heads, and readjusted their wigs, and planted their gold-headed canes on the floor with additional energy, while relating their experience in the Boerhaavian views of mechanical obstruction and *error loci*, and of lentor and viscidity of the fluids as the cause of fever and inflammation! And the pulse—did not at all experience, they might be heard to exclaim, confirm the indications, in this sense, which it furnished? Boerhaave himself, repeating the language of Hippocrates, had said, *experientia fallax;* and the fallacies of the great Professor of Leyden himself, furnished abundant evidence of the truth of the aphorism.

There are other important phenomena in which the heart performs a conspicuous part, and of which the pulse gives notice, but which are not explicable by a knowledge merely of the mechanism of the heart, and of the circulation. It was necessary to look for remoter agencies, by which this mechanism underwent such great and sudden transitions in its movements; as when it is disturbed by fever and jarred by strong emotion, or the irritations of other viscera. The pulse, under these circumstances, indicates great cardiac disturbance, but its revelations of more remote disorder were not always read in the proper sense. Something more than the blood, the normal stimulant of the heart, was to be studied: it was necessary to discover the connecting links between the heart, the central organ of the circulation, and the brain, the material organ of the mind, or great ganglionic centre of intellectual and emotional life, and also between the heart and the ganglionic centres and plexuses of nutritive or organic life. The nerves are these connecting links; and now, when we feel a pulse in a case of fever, we ought to be aware that we seek in the number and character of its beats an index, not only to the momentum with which the blood is impelled by the contractile power of the heart, but also the possible mental disturbance, and, still more certainly, the irritation or inflammation of a viscus, or it may be of several viscera or tissues, which, by a continual teazing, as it were, of the heart and the brain, keep up what we call fever. But the blood itself, in the artery beating beneath our fingers, has also its share in modifying the character of the pulse, not only by its quantity, but also by the varying proportions of its fibrin and blood globules; and also, in fevers, especially in typhus and the eruptive ones, by the introduction of a new and poisonous element, which displays its effects in sometimes exciting, but more frequently weakening the contractile and propelling power of the heart.

It is impossible, therefore, for the most exacting advocate of experience, and of reliance on simple facts as our guide in practice, to deny, while his fingers are on the pulse of his patient, who labors under fever, the necessity of passing in mental review the antecedent phenomena—hurried contraction of the heart, increased innervation on the heart from the nervous centres of animal and of nutritive life, and the probable change in the viscera or the tissues exciting these nervous centres; and finally, the altered properties of the blood, and, it may be, modification of the cellular coat of the vessel itself, by the changes in its reticulated nervous tissue. As a practical man, he is bound to carry in his mind all the facts; and if he draws inferences from them, he must reason on them, must form certain notions respecting their relations to each other, and their bearing on the subject immediately before him; in fine, he must theorize, not indeed at random, but according to the rules of sound medical logic. How little did experience, during the many centuries of the rule of the Galenical doctrines of sphygmology, add to the diagnostic value of the pulse in organic diseases of the heart! What strange experiences must have been recorded of the meaning to be attached to the feeble and exiguous pulse, and sometimes its entire absence, in dilatation of the heart with accompanying disease of the valves! What weakness of the nervous forces was inferred! What an amount of stimulation practised, at a time when the organ was laboring with double, but ineffectual power, owing to the derangement of its mechanism!

Let us, then, be ever ready to receive with an impartial and a kindly spirit any new fact of an experimenter, and not turn away from the plausible suggestions of a studious theorist, although they may conflict with our daily routine of observation, which we choose to dignify with the name of experience. But, in advocating the claims of science in medicine, as opposed to routine and empirical experience, and as combining doctrines and propositions which enable the practitioner to found upon them his rules for the treatment of his patients, we must not forget our legitimate line of study and logical argumentation. This will not be found in undue attachment to the opinions of men of general scientific enlightenment and over-estimation of novel acquisitions, nor in an adherence to the fallacious semblance of positivism, or exactness, which has crept, as if it were an integral part of medicine, into the train of microscopical and chemical methods of investigation.

But it is time that I should pass from these topics, which have come up incidentally, to the main subject of this address. I would here make a remark, in anticipation of some objections that may be brought to the strain of praise in which I shall indulge when speaking of the dignity of our profession, and the true nobility of many who have toiled in it. In our regular professional meetings we seldom indulge in mutual adulation. Our habit on these occasions is to scrutinize the real value of the facts and the suggestions which are brought before us for the diminution and cure of disease, or for the preservation and promotion of health. We are more anxious to keep up the standard of medical ethics and to enrich practical medicine than to elicit the plaudits of our fellows. Disguise it as we may, toil, incessant toil, and anxiety from first to last, are the fate of all who are engaged in the practice of medicine. It cannot, therefore, be deemed amiss, or if it be an error, it is an excusable one, to convert, occasionally, a commemorative address into a vehicle for words of encouragement and gratulation at the bright passages of our history, in order that we may with patience bear our inevitable trials, and, at the same time, be incited to emulous effort in the path which lies before us. The laurel is not gathered in fertile fields or flowery meadows, but on broken heights of rough ascent.

The present is an age in which not only the people of one nation, or even race, but mankind, the universal man, is "vexed with the love of change." It is an age not only of progress, but of transition, in which old ideas, like old armor and old tapestry, have become obsolete, and new ones are springing up in strange and often, it must be confessed, fantastic forms—not susceptible of classification, according to any known, or even conceivable system of psychology. But it is enough for the thoughtful and the benevolent to be aware that great changes are going on, and will go on, so that they may both protect themselves against extremes and excesses, as well as contribute their efforts towards giving a safe and useful direction to the new mental machinery, for the good of their fellow-men, whether of their own order or members of the great body politic.

Medicine, both in her scientific and professional aspects, is also being subjected to remarkable changes; but amid all of them, it becomes the duty of us who are votaries and worshippers at her altar, to see that no impious ceremonies, no witches' mummery shall take the place of the simple yet solemn rites, which the faithful in every successive age have always performed.

In forms we have conceded, or rather abandoned, a great deal. Let us not, in a too ready spirit of yieldingness, give up essentials. No longer is the physician recognized, in his daily round, by peculiarity of garb, manner, or language. The formal suit of black, the full bottomed wig, the shining knee and shoe-buckles, and the gold or ivory-headed cane, have disappeared, and with them the solemnity of manner, the measured and aphoristic fashion of speech which used to characterize our predecessors of the olden time. Something more has been given up besides. We are now content, as was said of Shakspeare, with a *little* Latin and *less* Greek, in place of the deep draughts which were quaffed by all who wished to be regarded as legitimate members of the schools of Hippocrates and Celsus.

But, although we may be less fluent in the language of Greece and of Rome than even our immediate predecessors, let us not forget, for a moment, the histories of those men who, from him of Cos down to a Jenner, a Rush, and a Pinel, have adorned the profession, and illustrated and ennobled humanity. If, proudly, we claim to be professionally descended from the Father of Medicine, and believe the language of an eminent writer, when he asserts that "the duties of a physician were never more beautifully exemplified than in his conduct, or more eloquently described than in his writings," we must be careful not to discredit the family by our failing to follow the example set by its illustrious founder. How much stronger still ought to be the desire to imitate our sires, when we know that every successive age down to the one we live in, has sent forth from our profession its heroes of humanity and dispensers of the richest lore! The elevated position assigned to us by an eminent scholar, when he says that "in erudition, in science, and in habits of deep and comprehensive thinking, the pre-eminence must be awarded, in some degree, to physicians," imposes on us correspondingly lofty obligations to continue to merit the praise thus spontaneously given. If, at this time, we are unable to erect pyramids which might excite the wonder of remote generations, let us at least build houses of shelter, in which fountains shall be introduced for the refreshment of the weary pilgrim and the traveller across the deserts of ignorance, and the thorny and briered wastes of prejudice and superstition.

Not only ought we to have the consciousness of our own strength, of the unbroken succession of great names, illustrated by great deeds, and of the dignity of the order to which we belong, but we must, also, for the sake of giving greater scope to our own well-meant efforts, impress our fellow-men, in all the walks of life, with our true position and aims. One of the first steps to accomplish our purpose will be to diffuse, and to render popular and familiar as household words, that portion of our rich and teeming literature in which are recorded the discoveries of the means of preventing diseases, and the disinterested and devoted efforts of those who have either perilled or laid down their lives to stay the march of pestilence, and to save their affrighted fellow-citizens, and apparently doomed victims, from its merciless assaults.

We do not study enough our own history; we are not familiar, as we ought to be, with the great deeds, the true heroism of our professional ancestors. They ought to form an integral part of the history of mankind, and find their place in the brightest passages of the history of every civilized people. The first dawn of civilization reveals the respect paid to medicine and to those who practised it, and with the advance in general knowledge, science, and refinement, there has always been an increase of this estimation. The Greeks, like the Egyptians, believed medicine to be of divine origin. Its humanizing and softening influences were typified in its tutelary deity, Apollo, being also regarded as the god of poetry and of music. Gratitude for the numerous and extraordinary cures of disease performed by Esculapius did not stop short of his apotheosis, and of causing temples to be erected to him. Orpheus, the priest-poet, was also a physician. During this, the heroic age of Greece, we find mention made of the name of Ex, who was of the school of Chiron the Centaur, and physician and surgeon to the expedition of the Argonauts, which we are afraid must incur the imputation of having been somewhat of the filibustering character, similar to that of the restless and buccaneering spirits of the present day, or to that of the age of Queen Elizabeth, as represented by Sir Francis Drake and his associates. Another and more celebrated pupil of Chiron, and also one of the Argonauts, was Hercules, who is more thought and spoken of for feats of great bodily prowess than as a reformer of abuses and ills, which interfered with the safety and the health of the people of the different countries that he visited. Viewed in this light, he is among the earliest of our medical heroes, and a great sanitary reformer. In fact, we must look on him as the symbol of the history of Grecian civilization, more particularly in its physical aspects, as in his draining of morasses and lakes, digging of canals, extirpating of forests and of the wild beasts that infested them. The story of Hercules destroying the Hydra, the many-headed monster, near Lake Lerna, is an allegory intended to show that he, or rather the first authors of civilization personified in him, cleared and drained the Peloponnesus, and so exposed the previously marshy soil to the sun as to cause a thorough desiccation. In another of his twelve labors, the cleansing of the Augean stable, we see the symbolic representation of accumulated filth, and at the same time a resort to the most judicious means for abating the nuisance. If Hercules had been the representative of mere animal strength, as he is too commonly regarded, he would have set about the task imposed on him by Eurystheus, in scavenger fashion, by digging up and shovelling out the accumulated filth in the stables of Augeas. But the demi-god, endowed with the higher qualities of mind, had recourse to a more complete and rational process, which consisted in turning the river Alpheus, or some say the Peneus, through the stable, and thus carrying off the accumulations of thirty years, and at the same time thoroughly cleansing the receptacle of so many abominations. How many cities at the present day have their foul corners, worse than the Augean stable, without, however, a Hercules or even any of the Heraclidæ, his descendants, to cleanse and purify them! An entire river cannot often be diverted into a new channel for the purpose, but a portion of its water ought always to be distributed in minor and artificial streams, so that the streets should be washed by hose irrigation, and the contents of the sewers carried off by flushing, if a perennial flow cannot be obtained for this purpose.

The separation of history from myth took place in the persons of Machaon and Podalirius, reputed sons of Esculapius. They were the last of the heroic age who figured both as warriors and physicians, for such was their part at the siege of Troy. Thus

Homer, in his Iliad, Book II., when giving a catalogue of the Grecian ships, tells,

> "In thirty sail the sparkling waves divide
> Which Podalirius and Machaon guide;
> To these his skill their parent god imparts
> Divine professors of the healing arts."

Henceforward we are to meet with medical men in their true and appropriate relations to the world, as heroes of humanity, as men who peril their lives, but it is always to save those of others: they combat not their fellow-men—but unseen, often unknown enemies, and are led into ambuscades from which are discharged more fearful and destructive missiles than man's devilish ingenuity has yet devised. In the philosophic and scrutinizing age of Greece, which succeeded the heroic, Plato is heard to say, that a good physician is only second to the Deity himself. This was the age of Hippocrates—that in which Pericles bore mild sway in Athens, and when philosophy, poetry, history, and the fine arts found their teachers and representatives, who have ever since been regarded, and to all appearances ever will be, as models for all time.

The opinion of Cato the Censor, and the strong prejudices of the Roman people during the first centuries of their history, against physicians, are often cited by those who would detract from the usefulness and merits of medicine. The enmity would seem, however, to have been directed more against the persons who practised it than against the art itself. The Romans were jealous of the intruding Greeks, and Cato kept no measures with the philosophers, orators, and physicians from Greece, when he accused them of corrupting the manners of the Romans. This rigid and rough moralist carried his animosity so far as to procure an edict for the expulsion of the two first-mentioned classes; but the physicians were spared. Something of personal and even professional rivalry may have had its share in Cato's persecution of the physicians, shall we call them the regular faculty then in Rome. He was the author of a work on domestic and veterinary medicine; and was in the habit of dosing with equal readiness and impartiality, and probably with equal success, his farm and house servants and domestic animals. He prepared the remedies himself: they were, we may presume, simples culled from his garden and fields, and were doubtless represented by him to be much more congenial with the patriotic stomachs of his countrymen than the exotic drugs brought and administered by the exotic Greeks. Unfortunately, however, for self-taught doctors, even of the Cato mould, there was a story at the time that the wife of the Censor fell a victim to his original and Roman method of medication. Pliny the elder, at a later period, was less consistent in his declamations against foreign physicians, inasmuch as he wrote a *Materia Medica* made up entirely from the works of the Greek authors. This early specimen of nativism may excite a smile of derision; but is it not of quite a mitigated character when compared with the exuberant manifestations of our own people in this way a few years ago? In Philadelphia they seemed to forget that a Girard, and in New York they were equally oblivious that an Astor had ever lived among them; the first to endow a palatial college for orphans—the second a library rich with the productions of the genius and learning of the natives of every country under heaven.

Voltaire pithily remarks, in reference to the obligations of mankind to physicians: to preserve and repair is almost equal to create. The Roman people let five hundred years pass without physicians. They were only occupied in destroying, and cared little for preserving life. How, adds this witty writer, did they make out at Rome, when a person was seized with a putrid fever, or had a fistula, or a pulmonary affection? He died. With the progress of civilization and of letters, the Romans acquired juster ideas of medicine and of its professors; a striking evidence of which is furnished in the language of the eloquent and philosophic Cicero: that nothing brings men nearer to the gods, than by giving health to their fellow-creatures.

But why should we seek to emblazon our escutcheon, by bringing on its field the symbolical figures of the mythology of Greece and Rome? Receiving humbly our shield from him who has been called the Great Physician, and taking him as our head and guide, let us rather enrich its scroll with mottoes from sacred writ, than care to decorate its mantling, crests, or supporters, with the creations of a truant fancy. The medical hero in Christian lands is not to be sought for in courts or in camps, nor in the busy and crowded haunts of the wealth-seeking; he is not on the Rialto or the Exchange, nor prominent at the polls; he is neither a demagogue, inflaming the passions of the multitude, nor a parasite, flattering the prejudices of the rich, or ministering to the caprices of those in power. He seldom finds a place in pageant or in festival; seldom is called upon

2

to add his voice to the peans of victory. He passes through the crowd often unknown, uncared for, unless indeed it may be when he meets the face of one radiant with smiles, whom he had visited but a short time before, prostrate on the bed of sickness, or hears his name uttered by another in a tone equivalent to saying, "God bless him!"

Where, then, shall we find our medical hero—what are his attributes, what his exploits? We shall soon see his fields of action, in which hundreds are gazing at him as a superior being, whose fiat determines their fate, either for recovery or for death. Unselfishness, sympathy, friendship, are words ever grateful to the ear of humanity; they represent feelings dear to our common nature; and although genius may sometimes not know them, and the intellect fail to appreciate their intrinsic value, yet they must always form a part of a truly great and noble character. They are in continual exercise among physicians, and are the chief constituents of medical heroism. I shall now proceed to prove the truth of this averment, and begin by adducing a rare instance of self-abnegation and friendship derived from common or extra professional life.

A Frenchman of some literary celebrity, whose name I cannot recall, was seized with a violent, and, as he rightly believed, a fatal disease. His cherished friend coming into the room, in which at the moment there were several visitors, was called to his bedside, and addressed in a low tone of voice, in the following words: "Send away these people, and come and nurse me yourself. You know that my disease is contagious, and you alone, as a true friend, are the only one entitled to expose himself for me." The request of the sick man was complied with; the many inquiring visitors retired, and the privileged friend took his post at the bedside, and remained there until the death of him who had given such unusual proof of his confidence. This friend soon after sickened and died of the same disease.

Sentiment and song might be, probably have been, enlisted to celebrate so touching a proof of disinterested and devoted friendship. I would not detract from its merit by the remark that a *true* man is bound to risk fortune and life, aye, reputation itself, for his friend. In the present warmth of his own feelings, in the reminiscences of past confidential intercourse and of innumerable kind and loving acts, he forgets himself, he sees no danger and hesitates at no sacrifice in the service of his friend. If he reason for a moment he will say to himself: "I, too, would be sure of receiving from him, if the occasion required it, a like proof of regard for me and of forgetfulness of himself."

But in what terms, by what epithets shall we designate him who, without any such genial incentives, without any expectation of possible reciprocity, or hope of applause, and certainly without any of the returns for self-exposure which men might expect from men, goes about from day to day, and often too in the silent watches of the night, in a spirit of self-sacrifice of ease, comfort, health, and life itself, ministering relief to his pestilence-stricken and fever-tossed fellow creature, the inmate, it may be, of a garret or a cellar of some wretched tenement, in an infected court or alley, the approach to which is by a narrow passage, obstructed by accumulations of all kinds of refuse and impurities? Is this man a soldier, inured to scenes of carnage and death, whose vocation makes him regardless of danger, and who, although he may be detailed on the forlorn hope, knows that if he fall, his name will be recorded in the Gazette, and his wife and children receive perhaps a pension? Or is he a salaried official, who, for a certain pecuniary return and perquisites, is discharging a prescribed and covenanted duty? O, no! This simple-minded man, who goes about his duty for duty's and humanity's sake, is only a *doctor*, one of a class at whom every witling is privileged to fling a sarcasm, and whom every venal quack may accuse of selfishness, and greediness of gold.

"During the famine fever of 1847 in Ireland, one hundred and seventy-eight Irish medical practitioners, exclusive of medical pupils and army surgeons, died, being a proportion of nearly seven per cent., or one in every 1.5 medical practitioners, in a single year." Some persons may say that physicians who thus expose themselves and who pay the penalty of death for their exposure, are encouraged by the expectation of pecuniary advantage in the shape of fees. We must all wish that they had such inducements; they could readily afford to forego a part of their reputation for benevolence and disinterestedness, in consideration of their receiving that by which they could support their wives and children, or an aged parent, or a lone sister. But it so happens, that in all epidemic and pestilential diseases, the chief privation and dangers incurred by medical men are in their attendance on the poor, the needy and the destitute, and not seldom the dissolute, who have no claim on them by prior acquaintance or the most trivial service, and from whom they receive no fees, and often no thanks, or the slightest token of gratitude.

The greater part of the mortality among the Irish physicians was caused by their attendance on hospitals, and on the poor and half-starved occupants of cabins and hamlets, the air of which was often in such a state of concentrated virulence as to strike on the nervous system with almost the force and suddenness of the electric aura. And shall no page in history, no lines in poetry, celebrate the heroic deeds of these devoted men, who must have battled with a stouter heart against an unseen enemy than Leonidas and his Spartan band against the Persian host, or the Light Brigade in its daring and rash charge on the serried Russian lines at Inkerman? These heroes of humanity ought to be honored with a monumental inscription, even though it were couched in as brief phrase as that over the remains of the Athenians under Miltiades—

"They fought at Marathon."

Some years ago many physicians of the city of New York lost their lives in their attendance on the newly-arrived emigrants—strangers who might, indeed, claim the rights of hospitality, but not at the cost of the lives of their benefactors.

Two of the most remarkable and destructive pestilences on record occurred, the first in the early part, the second near the end of the last century. I refer to the plague of Marseilles in 1720, and the yellow fever of Philadelphia in 1793, in both of which the medical profession furnished more than its proportion of martyrs in the cause of humanity. History has done justice, but not more than justice, to the apostolic labors and devotedness of the good and pious Bishop of Marseilles, M. De Belzunce, during the entire period of the plague in that city. It has failed, however, as usual, to record in appropriate terms the labors and services, without fee or reward, of its physicians; and still worse, it has been falsified, so as to make it appear that the city was deserted by these, the guardians of her health, and her defenders against disease. Doctor Bertrand, author of the "History of the Plague at Marseilles," and one of the devoted band on that occasion, bears the following emphatic testimony to the courage and zeal of his colleagues: "Far from following the opinion of those who held that all attendance in case of plague should be left to the surgeons, to whom the physicians should be reserved as counsellors alone, they never shrank from personal attendance on the sick, but exposed their lives in endeavoring to give them succor, with the most undaunted courage and generosity. They were the first to face the danger of the contagion, going from street to street, from house to house, examining into everything, approaching the patients, feeling their pulses, examining their tumors, even dressing them with their own hands, if it appeared necessary; attending them, in short, with the same assiduity as could have been shown to a wealthy person, who was laboring under a common malady, and from whom they had expectations of a great reward. They never refused any service required of them, either in the hospitals, the city or the country; and all without any charge, except when they were obliged to go into the country, when some expense was unavoidable; but they never made any charge for their own trouble. All the recompense they received was contempt, and often insults, on the part of the people." This last sentence requires some explanation. It seems that the people became prejudiced against the physicians of the city, because these latter had declared the disease to be plague. But it was stupidly forgotten that, in dealing frankly and honestly with the public, the interests of the latter were alone consulted. The physicians knew well that their announcement of a terrible fact would at once drive away the wealthy from the city, and of course deprive them of the class of patients who would be able to pay them for their services, and that none but the poor would remain to receive medical attention. Had they, to humor the popular wish, concealed the nature of the disease at first, they would have been subjected, and with good reason, to public indignation, for withholding the truth, and lulling the people into a feeling of false security. The surgeons, who constituted a separate body, also acquitted themselves nobly, with the exception of a few deserters. Human nature is not always equal to the exigencies of time and place, even under the strongest appeals of humanity. Among the members of the community, outside of the professional ranks, it too often shows itself in a most cowardly fashion, under the plea of self-preservation. In the beginning of the plague at Marseilles, there were only four physicians, independently of the surgeons, to attend the sick in the different quarters of the city. Of these four, Mons. Bertrand had two attacks of the disease, from both of which he soon escaped; but, worn out with fatigue, and depressed by the loss of all his family, the members of which fell victims to the disease, in their endeavors to relieve and nurse the sick, this benevolent man was for some time disabled from resuming his professional duty. Let us add, that during the remainder of his life he was always regarded and treated with the greatest veneration by his fellow-citizens. Another of the small band died of the disease, and a third, exhausted by fatigue, and left without a servant, and almost the necessaries of life, was obliged for a while to go into the country. The surgeons were also reduced to a very small number; four or five only surviving out of thirty. Truly, then, was it said by the historian of the Marseilles plague, in reference to the situation and conduct of the professional men of the city: "And if, in the end, we were obliged to demand further assistance from other parts of the kingdom, it was not because those whose duty it was particularly to remain in the city had deserted their posts, but on account of the excess of the ravages made by the disease." In order to be able to appreciate in the smallest degree the services and exposures of the Marseilles physicians and surgeons at this time, we ought to have before our minds the frightful features of the disease, and the destitution and abandonment to which the people were reduced; the breaking up of every social tie among persons of all ranks, and the scenes of individual and family misery and suffering which everywhere met the eye of the medical and clerical visitors. During a season, these were almost the only persons who dared to quit their own abodes to solace and relieve their pest-stricken fellow-citizens.

There must be not a few still living in Philadelphia, among whose early reminiscences are some of the scenes of the memorable year of 1793, in which the city was so grievously afflicted with the yellow fever. Like the plague at Marseilles, this fever has had its historians, who described what they themselves saw, and actively participated in. If their pictures want the high finish which was imparted by the pen of a Thucydides to his description of the plague at Athens, they offer the largely compensating qualities of statistical and personal details. During the prevalence of this fatal epidemic, when all the bonds of society were loosened and the affections became cold and repellent, less concern, to use the language of an instructive chronicler of the disease, the late Matthew Carey, was felt for the loss of a parent, a husband, a wife, or an only child, than on other occasions could have been caused by the death of a servant, or even of a favorite lap-dog. "Acquaintances and friends avoided each other in the street, and only signified their regard by a cold nod. The old custom of shaking hands fell into such general disuse, that many persons shrank back with affright at the offer of the hand; a person with a crape, or any appearance of mourning, was shunned like a viper." In this more than beleaguered city—one more suffering than if it had been a prey to intestine strife, or than if gaunt famine had stalked through its streets unchecked—where were the medical soldiers, they who are always expected to be ready armed to combat disease in all its forms? With few exceptions, they were at their posts. How they battled with the raging pestilence, how they suffered, and how many of them fell in the struggle, is related in the pages of Rush, himself among the most distinguished of the devoted band. Within the short period of six weeks, during which this fever raged with the greatest violence, no less than ten physicians were carried off, and scarcely one of the survivors escaped an attack of the disease. At one time, as Dr. Rush relates, there were but three medical men (not counting, we must suppose, the French physicians, lately arrived from St. Domingo) who were able to do duty out of their houses. Medical students also, in imitation of their preceptors, and animated with a youthful zeal, which mastered the instinct of self-preservation, applied themselves devotedly to the relief of their suffering and dying fellow-citizens. Had the physicians of Phila-delphia in 1793 consulted their own safety, and availed themselves of the plea of its being their duty to follow the majority of the families of which they were the regular medical advisers, it were easy for them to have left the city with these latter, and others who fled, to the number of 17,000 persons, or more than a third of the entire population. In the history of the war of the Revolution, Dr. Benjamin Rush, as one of the signers of the Declaration of Independence, and Physician-General to the army, will always figure with the other worthies of that momentous period. But in the history of philanthropy he will occupy a still higher place, as one of the medical heroes who won his honors and enduring fame in the trying year of 1793, and in the other epidemic invasions of the yellow fever during the next twelve years. The fever of 1798 revived the terrors and the mortality of 1793, and, at the same time, gave opportunities for a display of heroic devotedness on the part of the physicians similar to that manifested in the latter year.

The outbreaks and fearful ravages of the yellow fever, which have occurred in other cities in the United States, down to the recent catastrophes from the same cause, by which Norfolk and Portsmouth, in Virginia, were so sorely afflicted, have been met by the same devotion to the public welfare, the same abnegation of self, and the same sacrifices, on the part of the physicians, wherever found.

Surprise is more frequently expressed at the escape of so many medical men from sickness and death, than at their falling victims during the prevalence of epidemic and malignant diseases. We are often asked: What are the means of prevention, what the charm by which we are able to walk abroad often unhurt, when death's arrows are flying in all directions around us? If some who thus wonder at the escape of physicians would sally out daily, with stout hearts and determined good-will, and visit the sick and the heavily laden, and administer to their necessities and wants in the way of little delicacies in food and drink, and of clothing when it is deficient; and, better perhaps than all, proffer pleasant words of encouragement and hope, they would readily understand the talismanic influence by which a physician is sustained in the consciousness that he is discharging a duty both to God and man. He is thus nerved to an exhibition of almost superhuman efforts, while he is continually risking his own life to save that of others. He ventures more than the bold swimmer, who plunges fearlessly into the rapid stream or the surging sea, to save a fellow-being from a watery grave. Without his going through the imposing forms of initiation and taking the vows of the knight-errant of former times, the physician pursues his vocation quietly and unostentatiously, succoring, not only the distressed of the fair sex, but also the poor, the distempered, the outcast of his own sex, who are often as forbidding in their persons as in their minds. There are attractive histories of chivalry. What restrains from writing a history of Medical Philanthropy? Why, for example, should not the discovery of vaccination, by Jenner, be as familiar a fact in school history as the invention of gunpowder by Roger Bacon, or the monk Schwartz? Had it been so, the women of England would have erected at least one other statue before that which they did raise to the conqueror at Waterloo. They would have been taught to dwell on their obligations to Jenner, who had found the means of saving them and their children, and their children's children, to future generations, from a loathsome, disfiguring, and constantly, in large proportion, a fatal disease. In dwelling on this picture, they would have been less prone to glorify Wellington, who had led their husbands, their fathers, and their sons to battle, to carnage, and to death. Why, under any aspect, should women give a preference to the destroyer over the conservator, even though that destroyer should be the victor in a hundred fights? No history has yet told us that the celebrated French surgeon, Ambrose Paré, ought to share with the Duke of Guise the honor of the successful defence of Metz, when that town was besieged by the Emperor Charles V. At a time when the garrison was nearly exhausted by continual fighting, and a scant supply of food, the French king sent word, exhorting it to hold out a little longer, and promised, as encouragement, to send them Ambrose Paré. The announcement had an electric effect, and the great surgeon was received within the walls of Metz with extravagant demonstrations of joy, as if he had come at the head of a powerful army to raise the siege. The soldier no longer feared wounds when he knew that he could procure Ambrose Paré to dress them, or even to direct their dressing by others.

Still more animated must have been the feeling of the whole French army in Egypt under Napoleon, or, as he was then more commonly called, Buonaparté, towards the chiefs of the medical and surgical staff. The troops, after witnessing the ravages of the plague, became alarmed and disheartened; and men who had never feared an enemy in the field of battle, now shrank with horror from the touch and breath of a sick companion in the quiet tent. To the general such a state of things was worse than the loss of a battle. In vain were the soldiers told that their fears were without foundation; in vain were they addressed in the language of encouragement and hope. Something must be done, either to change their belief or to appeal strongly to their imagination. Accordingly, Napoleon himself conversed freely with the patients who were stricken with the plague, and touched their bodies, and even sometimes performed the part of a nurse by raising them up and supporting them in their beds, in order to prove that there was no danger, and that the disease was not contagious. These traits of cool courage are recorded by every historian of the wars of the French Revolution; but few have thought it worth while to notice the more daring exploit of Desgenettes, one of the physicians of the army of Egypt. He not only touched and handled the bodies of those who had sickened with the plague, but he inoculated himself with their blood and other fluids. On another occasion, after Berthollet had expressed his belief that the poison of the plague was conveyed into the body by means of the saliva, a patient, dying of this disease, begged that Desgenettes would take a part of what was left of the draught that had been prescribed for him. Without hesitation, or betraying the slightest emotion, Desgenettes took the cup from the sick man, filled it up, and drank its contents entire.

If we believe that the design of the two—the military leader and the physician—was the same at this time, viz., to infuse confidence into the minds of the soldiers, it is not difficult to decide to which of them should be awarded the palm for this daring exposure of his life. Napoleon felt that all his prospects of conquest and fame would be clouded unless he could restore the sinking courage of his army; and hence he readily incurred some danger to secure so important an end. Desgenettes was buoyed up by no such aspirations. His incentives were humanity and a search after truth. Why not make this fine trait of the physician more prominent than that of the soldier in a school history? A small volume, consisting of incidents of this nature, might be prepared and introduced into the public schools. I would offer some additional facts and reflections, in the way of contributing a chapter to a work of this kind.

While French medicine was thus represented in Egypt by the calm and self-possessed Desgenettes, who was at the head of the medical staff, French surgery shone with, perhaps, still greater lustre in the person of the eminent Larrey, who, by his invention of the light ambulance for carrying off the wounded from the field of battle, won the affection of the soldier, and by this act alone becomes entitled to honorable mention in the annals of philanthropy. From the burning sands of Egypt, to the ice-bound rivers and snow-covered plains of Russia, in Poland, in Prussia, in Saxony, in Austria, in Italy, in Spain, and in France itself, Larrey not only encountered all the vicissitudes of climate and season, and the hardships incident to camp-life, but he was constantly engaged in the discharge of his arduous duties as field and hospital surgeon, fearless of personal risk, and intent only on affording the promptest relief to those placed under his care. He did not wait at a safe distance from the field of battle for the wounded to be brought to him; he was found in the midst of the wounded, the dying and the dead, ready and resolute, and always self-possessed; operating with equal promptitude and skill on those whom he could first reach or who were most in need of his services, and not caring for the rank of the prostrate man before him. Instances are recorded in which Larrey and his assistants, carried away by their professional, and, shall it be said, in part, also, their national enthusiasm, were seen giving their attentions to the wounded near the imminent and deadly breach itself, amidst a shower of destructive missiles which were carrying wounds and death to those around them. Larrey was exposed to the same fire under which Caffarelli, Lannes, Arrighi, Beauharnais, and many others fell, either wounded or never to rise again. After the long-contested and bloody battle of Eylau, in Polish Prussia, between the French and Russians, the Emperor Napoleon found Larrey standing in the snow, under a slight canopy of branches of trees, engaged in dressing the wounded; and on his passing by the same place, at the same hour, on the following day, he saw the indefatigable surgeon still occupied as before. In this way did Larrey spend twenty-four hours uninterruptedly, except in the few minutes snatched for a hurried repast. We have all heard or read of displays of zeal—religious, fanatical, patriotic, and amorous, but seldom has there been recorded a finer example of benevolent zeal spent on so good and useful a purpose.

Larrey was with the Grand Army, which, under Napoleon, invaded Russia, and occupied Moscow. It has been said that the burning of that capital brought with it the extinction of the French empire as such. From that epoch the star of Napoleon began to be dimmed, and continued to give a flickering light, until, in a short time, it set forever behind the rock of St. Helena. Larrey participated in the sufferings of the terrific retreat from Moscow, in which all discipline was forgotten, and soldiers, losing even the semblance of men, were changed into livid spectres, or trembling shadows, decked in fantastic rags, following gaunt famine as their leader. But even at such a time as this, when the better sentiments of human nature seemed, like all the objects of external nature, to be frozen up, the soldiers did not forget their friend, their oft-tried benefactor. A river had to be crossed by a detachment of the army, for which two bridges were constructed. But not the troops alone were hurrying over. With the soldiers, and horses, and artillery, crowded on unhappy fugitives from Moscow with their wives, and children, and baggage. In the advancing multitude Larrey was recognized; and immediately a thousand voices exclaimed: "Let us save him who has saved us. Let him come forward." All stop at once in their wild rush. Larrey is allowed to reach the bridge, and he is suddenly raised in the arms of the nearest soldiers and passed from hand to hand, until he is, in this manner, carried entirely across the river. He is saved just at the moment when the bridge gives way, and a crowd of human beings, of both sexes and all ages, together with horses, and cannon, and military wagons, are precipitated into the half-frozen stream beneath; most of them never to reach its banks, never to breathe again. Among these last was a young mother, who held up her infant above her head, as a mute but touching appeal to some one to save it. A soldier took it when she was about to sink, and her last struggles were soothed by the consciousness that her child was saved.

Larrey, ever faithful to Napoleon, for whom he cherished a feeling of strong personal attachment, followed him to Waterloo, where he was wounded, and made prisoner by the Prussians, and was on the point of being shot by his exasperated enemies. He was, however, happily recognized by the Prussian surgeon-major, who was about to put the fatal band over his eyes, and he was then conducted to General Bulow, and afterwards to Marshal Blucher, whose son he had formerly saved from almost inevitable death. Larrey was soon set at liberty, and was sent at first to Louvain, whence he repaired to Brussels, and made the first use of his returning strength in visiting the hospitals, crowded with the wounded of both the victors and the vanquished, to whom he gave equally his services. At the solicitation of the commanders of the allied armies in Paris, he is recalled to that capital, and is once more restored to his family, which for many days had believed him to be dead. Under the Restoration he was deprived of his pension and the decoration of the Legion of Honor, but still preserved his post of surgeon-in-chief at Gros Caillou, the hospital of the Royal Guard. On the last of the three days of July, 1830, in which the troops of the line had suffered so terribly from the fires behind the barricades and from the houses, his hospital was surrounded by an exasperated crowd, uttering all kinds of threats. Larrey made his appearance, and addressed them in the following terms: "What do you mean? Whom do you dare to threaten? Know that these sick men are mine; that it is my duty to defend them, and yours to respect yourselves in respecting the unfortunate." This timely firmness put a stop to further attempts at violence, and the noisy troop withdrew, taking with them the arms from which they had no longer anything to fear. This brave and good man retained all his energies to an advanced age. In 1842, when he was in his seventy-sixth year, he made an official tour of inspection of the hospitals of Algeria, and at Bonn he performed the operation of amputating the arm of an Arab. Can we better terminate these brief notices of Larrey, which exhibit him in the light of a true hero of humanity, than by a mention of the bequest of Napoleon of twenty thousand dollars to him as the most virtuous man whom he had ever known?—a higher eulogy even than that paid by the Roman emperor to Galen, when he sent a medal with the inscription: IMPERATOR ROMANORUM IMPERATORI MEDICORUM.

We change the scene, and this time it opens in the Crimea, after the battle of the Alma, in which the Russians were defeated by the allied troops of France and England, in 1854. You have read of the feats of valor displayed on both sides on that bloody field—the sweeping fire of the artillery, the daring charge of cavalry, the deadly encounter of the columns of infantry, when men met men with bayonets crossed, in the mixed excitement of animal passion, national rivalry, and the thirst for honor and distinction. The names of St. Arnaud and Raglan, the victorious generals, were suddenly sounded and sung in both hemispheres, and they took at once their places in history. But the real hero, the saviour, not the destroyer, appeared on the day after the battle, unheralded by drum or trumpet, a devoted, and to all appearances a doomed volunteer in the cause of humanity. The allied forces were under the military obligation of advancing rapidly on Sebastopol in pursuit of the retreating Russians, and in doing so to leave 750 wounded of the enemy behind them on the field of battle. "Who," to use the words of an English medical journal, "is that single individual who, of all the host that is marching away from the scene of its late triumph, is still to be found upon that blood-stained field? And what is the errand on which he is engaged, thus alone among his enemies, watching the retreating forms of his friends, his countrymen, and gathering up his courage as best he may, to undertake the duties which, in obedience to the dictates of humanity, it had become his duty to perform? This most painful and desolate duty was imposed on himself by Dr. Thomson, of the 44th Regiment, a native of Cromarty, in the northern part of Scotland, the birthplace also of Hugh Miller, of the Red Sandstone fame. Provided with some rum, biscuit, and salt meat, he was left with his charge; his only companion a private soldier, acting as his servant. This was indeed a forlorn prospect. Could he escape from the savage assaults of the marauding Cossacks, a party of whom had ruthlessly destroyed a villa not many miles off, on the road to Balaklava, the residence, too, of a Russian country surgeon or physician, who had been obliged to make a hasty retreat? Even the patients themselves, whether under the influence of fever, caused by their wounds, or by mere brutal ferocity, had fired at or stabbed the humane individuals who were then dressing their wounds. Five days, however, did Surgeon Thomson pass in the midst of such a people, whose language was unknown to him, without any companion but his soldier-servant. Often were these two Englishmen obliged to extricate the wounded from beneath the dead before their gashes could be healed, and also to bury the dead because of the pestilential smell arising from the mutilated carcasses. Their scanty supply of food was about to fail them. On the dreaded approach of a swarm of Cossacks, 340 wounded men, who five days previously lay in helpless agony on the ground, walked away with Surgeon Thomson to the shore, and, after overwhelming their deliverer from death with expressions of gratitude, sailed for Odessa. The surgeon himself escaped from the Cossacks, and reached the English head-quarters on the 4th of October, but died of cholera the next day, worn out by the hardships he had undergone. Surely," adds the English journalist, "James Thomson, of the 44th Regiment, has earned a monument, for in his own noble character were united the physician's skill, the soldier's courage, and the Christian's humanity."

Of the strange events by which the present century has been distinguished—long and devastating wars, revolutions, pestilence, and famine—none have been so unexpected and sudden in its inception, and followed by atrocities so far beyond human belief, and, until then, beyond all that imagination could picture, as the Sepoy mutiny and rebellion in India. The numerous medical officers belonging to the British armies in that country furnished their full quota, not only in their own persons, but in their wives and children, to the victims of that horrible outbreak. They did more: they furnished at one hour a contingent of brave soldiers in battle and siege; and in the next, showed themselves the heroes of humanity, who disregarded danger and fatigue in the exercise of their legitimate vocation—the saving of lives, and the cure of the sick and the maimed. General Whitlock makes honorable mention of Surgeon Bradley, who attended his wounded under a heavy fire. The Victoria Cross, the highest reward of the brave, was conferred on Surgeon Antony Dickson Horne, of the 90th Regiment, "for persevering bravery and admirable conduct in charge of the wounded men left behind the column, when the troops, under the late Major-General Havelock, forced their way to the residency of Lucknow, on September 29, 1857." The escort left with the wounded were forced into a house, in which they defended themselves till it was set on fire. They then retreated to a shed, a few yards from it, and in this place continued to defend themselves for more than twenty two hours, until relieved. At the last only six men and Mr. Horne remained to fire. Of four officers, who were with the party, all were wounded, and three are since dead. The conduct of the defence during the latter part of the time devolved, therefore, on Mr. Horne, and to his active exertions previously to being forced into the house, and his good conduct throughout, the safety of any of the wounded and the successful defence are mainly to be attributed." Assistant Surgeon Bradshaw received, also, the Victoria Cross for acts of bravery of the same date and place, and as associated with Surgeon Horne in the same gallant services.

In the massacre at Cawnpoor, one of the most terrific scenes by which the Indian mutiny was marked, a number of medical men fell victims to the savage fury of the Sepoys. Surgeon Kirk was shot in the presence of his wife, who pleaded, with true womanly devotion, to give her life for his. The high-tiled roof of the General Hospital was the only mark open to the enemy, by reason of which all their guns and mortars were directed against it. An assistant surgeon, writing from Cawnpoor after the siege, says: "Three round-shot passed through my hospital roof, but fortunately, although bringing down plenty of tiles and dirt, no one was injured. Bullets continually pattered against the hospital walls; but all high up, as the earthworks protected the lower part." During the first of the six days in which this surgeon was in the intrenchments, he amputated eight limbs, and dressed more than eighty wounded men; he himself scarcely knowing night from day, and eating beef and biscuit, and drinking tea and water when he could get a chance. The siege of Lucknow by the rebel Sepoys is full of instances of heroic fortitude and bravery, in which medical men largely participated, acting the double part, as occasion called for, of combatants and surgeons. Assistant Surgeon Henry Bartram was shot down at the gate of the Residency, within a few hundred yards of where his wife was expecting him. At a subsequent date, Dr. Darby died from a gunshot wound, received in action, in the advance on Lucknow, under Sir Colin Campbell, now Lord Clyde.

It was indeed time for the English Government to awake to a sense of the real position and services of the medical staff, in both military and maritime forces. Intelligent men, not warped in their opinions by the prejudices of routine and old customs, must always have been at a loss to discover any reasonable argument, or even a plausible pretext, for the indignity with which the medical officer was so long treated in both branches of the service, not only in England, but in the United States, by their being refused equivalent rank with other military and naval officers, and the same official privileges as these latter. I will not argue the question at this time, for fear of being betrayed into expressions which might savor of that arrogance on our part for which those in the army and navy, who have opposed the demands of justice to our profession, should be pointedly rebuked. There are military officers, however, of high station and widespread fame, who have learned to appreciate, at their true value, the services of medical men in the public service. Conspicuous among these advocates is Sir de Lacy Evans, than whom no man stands higher in the British army, for his gallantry, bordering on rashness, his long and brilliant services, and his strategetic skill. General Evans made a speech in the House of Commons (June 21, 1849) in which he pointed out the losses that the British troops suffered during the last long war with France, and the hardships and exposures to all the chances of war, including loss of life itself, by medical officers in active service; and he referred at the same time to the distinctions and praises awarded to them by Napoleon. He closed by submitting a resolution with a view of affirming:—

"That the sanitary efficiency of armies must, in a great measure, depend on the ability, energy, and zeal of the medical officers attached to them.

"That the history of every war proves that this class of officers have been killed, wounded, or made prisoners, the nature of their duties unavoidably exposing them to these casualties.

"And that, as they share in the dangers and fatigues of war, as well as in some of its most essential responsibilities, it is not expedient or just that they should be excluded from a share of honorary distinction or reward, in proportion to their relative services."

General Evans, in the course of his speech, dwelt more particularly on the losses encountered during the Peninsular war. The summary result proves, as we learn from him, that during the six years' contest about 500,000 men were successively sent back, restored to efficiency from the hospitals, to resume their duties in the ranks. "Can it be possible," adds the speaker, "to adduce stronger evidence of the weighty and fearful responsibilities, labors, and anxieties which devolved on medical officers in the field? A disciplined soldier, when brought before the enemy, has already cost the State a large sum. However adequate may be the original numerical strength provided for a service, the preservation of the lives, health, and efficiency of the troops, so far as within the reach of art, must always, in contests of importance, intimately affect the combinations of the general, the termination of wars, and the national resources. For the adequate execution of such duties, science, courage, energy, and an ardent devotion to the service, must obviously be requisite. Money alone will not suffice for these qualities; a generous and honorable ambition must also be satisfied; but with this a treatment of indignity or contempt is incompatible."

Sir de Lacy Evans stated that, although he was more familiar, of course, with the case of the army medical officers, and that the motion he should submit referred verbally to the military department, yet substantially the cases of both services rest on the same basis.

Let us hope that the American Government will not be backward in placing the medical officers of the army and navy on a permanent footing of rank, nor niggard in awarding them their proper share of honorary distinction and reward.

Any record of the feats of the benevolent daring which enters so largely into the composition of medical heroism would be incomplete, and want its brightest page, that did not include a notice of a professional brother and a countryman, and yet more, a fellow-citizen—a Philadelphian, whose name and whose fame are now

3

world wide, while his remains rest on the banks of our own Schuylkill. Need I mention Dr. Elisha Kent Kane? His noble deeds, his chivalrous philanthropy, his Christian faith, buoying him up amidst dangers and privations at which the stoutest hearts might have quailed, are too fresh in your memory to require any commemoration of mine. Happily, there is no room for engaging in this pleasing duty, did it even lie more directly in my way, now that the world has the benefit of Dr. Elder's appreciative and well-written volume.

Another passage for the records of Medical Heroism, and I have done :—

The name of Howard is everywhere celebrated, and praised in terms of warm gratitude, as the reformer of prison abuses and prison cruelties. It has obtained a place in the history of the world's progress. The name of Pinel is not, I am afraid, familiar even to the medical world; and it is still less to the world at large, as that of a physician, who, both by personal services and earnest teaching brought about a reform in the management and discipline of Asylums for the Insane, which may now be properly regarded one of the strongest proofs of advanced civilization. If a proper sympathy and sentiment for humanity and justice have been enlisted by the benevolent Englishman, in what light ought we to regard the services of the equally benevolent Frenchman, who reminded men of their duties to the Providence stricken, but irresponsible insane? Excuse might be found for vindictive harshness to the criminal who has made war on society; but where is the extenua· tion for more deliberate cruelty, practised so long and so generally on those unfortunate beings, bereft of their reason, many of whom, but a short time before, had been the delight of the social circle, and cherished members of the family?

When we think of the old Bedlams and Hospitals for the Insane, in which not only the raving maniac, but the melancholy monomaniac was confined, and in which the only sounds were those of the clanging chain, the echoing lash, and the mingled cries and vociferations of the brutal keepers and the infuriated inmates; and then look abroad over the better portions of the civilized world, including our own favored land, and see the many noble edifices erected for the reception and treatment of this class of unfortunate fellow-beings, we feel that we live in an age not only of progress, but of real improvement; one in which humanizing influences are more active and diffused than they ever were before. The contrast between the present and the past in this particular, while it should prompt all to the liveliest manifestations of gratitude, ought, undoubtedly, to find a place in general history, in which proper credit would be awarded to our profession, so many members of which have imitated, in their official position as superintendents of Insane Asylums, the noble example set by Pinel at the Bicêtre and the Salpêtrière.

That was indeed a critical moment in the life of Pinel, and in the history of benevolent trials for the mitigation of human suffering, when he resolved to test the correctness of his principles of non-restraint, by holding direct personal intercourse with a violent maniac, whose chains and fetters he had previously directed to be removed. The trial was entirely successful. After an eager gaze and a movement, as if preparatory to a tiger-like spring on his visitor, who had just entered his cell, the unfortunate being saw eyes beaming with kindness and placid features, expressing benignity and good-will. Soon his own countenance underwent a change; the mere brute was once again a human being; and when the tones of affectionate inquiry reached his ear, and the hand of greeting was extended towards him, he could only answer and reciprocate by shedding tears, the fountains of which had long been dried up by the fiery furnace of maddened feelings, wrought to fury by angry menace and brutal punishment. From this moment the cure of the poor maniac, which had been before regarded as hopeless, was begun, and terminated in entire restoration to health and reason.

After the inquiring visitor has been taken through a modern lunatic asylum, and traversed its spacious corridors, and has looked into its neat and cheerful dormitories, and is then taken to the saloon and the lecture-room, and the rooms for social meetings and amusements, and is farther shown, out of doors, the extensive grounds for exercise and recreation, all under the direction of the medical superintendent, the presiding genius of the place, he gives utterance to his conviction by exclaiming: "After all, madness is not so dreadful an infliction, when it is met, controlled, and so often conquered by the harmonious union of medical science, philanthropic vigilance, and ingenuity, and, at fitting times, the soothing balm of religious counsel and exhortation."

In the vestibule of every modern lunatic asylum, the visitor might naturally expect to see a statue of Pinel, unless he should think at the moment of the inscription on St. Paul's Cathedral, London, in allusion to its celebrated architect, Sir Christopher Wren: "If you ask for a monument, look around you."

May I ask you to indulge me while making a few remarks in connection with the name of Pinel? We hear a great deal, in these days of specialties, of the necessity of a physician or surgeon, as the case may be, devoting himself to the study and practice of a particular branch, if he looks to doing the most good to others— and the most benefit to himself, in a pecuniary point of view. Without engaging in a discussion of the question, I feel myself anthorized to assert, that a specialty ought, like the shaft and capital of a column in a building, to rest on an enduring and highly finished support, such as would allow of our raising on it the final and more distinctive part in a great variety of styles. Thus, for instance, as the atticurgic base is the favorite one in architecture for columns of the Ionic, Corinthian, and Composite orders, so ought an accurate knowledge of the several parts of medical science, at least of their essential features, be the base for raising on it a specialty. Wanting this support, the practitioner of any specialty is reduced to the level of a small literary artisan, who is unable to see the application of a general law, or the relations of his branch to the other branches of science. It is an exceedingly equivocal compliment, something like the knocking a man down with a hearty slap on the back as a friendly salutation, to say of a physician: He is a good doctor, or is famous for curing diseases of the eye or the ear, but he is ignorant of everything else. Not in such language dare men speak of the distinguished members of our profession, who were accomplished scholars in general literature and science, and at the same time rich in medical lore, while ready with all the resources of medical practice.

Of this number was Pinel. Soon after his arrival in Paris from Montpelier, where, and at Toulouse, he had prosecuted his medical studies, he became a contributor to the *Journal of Paris*, and wrote on medicine, natural philosophy, and political economy. His attention was also directed to anatomy and surgery, on which he wrote interesting papers. A little later we find him contributing to the *Encyclopédie Méthodique*, translating Cullen, and editing Baglivi. He was not content with being a teacher in these ways; he was also a learner, still adding to his stores of knowledge, by attending the lectures of his friend, Desfontaines, on Botany, and of D'Arcet and Fourcroy on Chemistry.

Was the mind of Pinel distracted by these various studies and labors? Did he continue to be a mere man of books, a book-worm, unfitted to make a direct and practical application of his powers and attainments to higher purposes, or, at any rate, to some useful specialty? Let not your men of mere facts without method, and of observation without reflection, triumph in such a belief. Pinel had undergone an intellectual training which fitted him for the active discharge of the most responsible duties, just as gymnastic exercises and field sports prepare a man to endure the fatigues of a campaign, and to win honors by his courage and presence of mind in the hour of battle.

When a man is thus trained, as Pinel was, by prolonged, and, at the same time, various study, a slight circumstance will give direction and application to his future labors. Grief for the loss of a dear young friend, who wandered into the woods in a fit of mental derangement, and was torn to pieces by wolves, fixed the attention of Pinel on the subject of insanity; and to its elucidation, and the treatment of those suffering under that dread malady, he devoted the best part of his subsequent life.

Here we may be allowed to pause for a moment, and ask, whether Pinel would have been better prepared for the discharge of his duties as superintendent of an insane asylum, by his having spent the years of his noviciate in a similar institution, and become wedded to a routine of hardships and cruelty to the inmates, in ignorance of the mind, except in its deformities, than by the prior exercise of all his intellectual faculties in the manner already pointed out. The answer might, I think, be left with a jury of practical, which most of the time means practising physicians, even though they may have had only a slight sprinkling of humane letters, and a very elementary knowledge of the philosophy of mind. But Pinel's labors and learning were spread over a wide field of medical science. For many years his *Nosographie Philoso-phique* was the standard work in France on pathology and thera-peutics. In its perusal Bichat found the germs of his doctrine and division of the tissues, which were expanded into their full measure and harmonious proportions in his celebrated *General Anatomy.* Pinel's *Treatise on Mental Alienation* was of a subsequent date. In addition to the merits of this work in its facts and lucid arrangement, it is pervaded by a vein of pure morality, and is full of valuable suggestions to parents and teachers for the guidance of youth, and for protecting them against temptations which, if yielded to, often unseat reason from her throne.